Before her mind realized what she was doing, her body and heart had already made the call.

Her school bag, with his gift of roses, slid off her shoulder as she let go of his arm to, finally, put her own arms around him. She could reach his shoulders, his neck; she had to stand on tiptoes and force his head down with all her might. And it worked.

She kissed him.

She didn't think about it anymore. She just moved as she had always wanted to. She ran her hands over his back and his thick hair; she used her tongue to taste him, his lips, the inside of his mouth. The rest of her followed; her chest and her hips pressed against him, wanting more, maybe at least for him to touch her, too.

He understood.

She knew as much when he came to life, knowing exactly what she wanted, what she needed.

SHIRLEY SIATON

A NOVELLA

ANGEL

SHE ONLY EVER SAW AND
LOVED HIM IN THE SHADOWS.

ANGEL

A Novella

Copyright © 2023 Shirley Siaton-Parabia

ISBN 978-1-96-105203-1 (pbk)
ISBN 978-6-21-837413-3 (Kindle)

First Edition, August 2023

Inky Sword Book Publishing
Barangay Quezon, Arevalo, Iloilo City 5000
Republic of the Philippines
inkysword.com

CONTENT WARNINGS

Warnings for explicit content, mild profanity
and references to violence.

Recommended for mature readers 18 years old
and above.

PLAYLIST

"My Heart"
Paramore

"Secret Love Song"
Little Mix & Jason Derulo

"Dusk till Dawn"
Zayn & Sia

"Going Under"
Evanescence

"Hero"
Enrique Iglesias

"Put Your Arms Around Me"
Texas

To Peter

TABLE OF CONTENTS

ACKNOWLEDGMENTS

I am very grateful to *Glitter Magazine Philippines*, the very first national publication that gave me and my fiction a chance to take center stage. It has been decades, but I have always held this opportunity in the highest esteem.

My gratitude to the fabulous team at Artscandare Design for the gorgeous book cover, to Rein Geronimo for the line art pieces featured at the beginning and end of this novella, and to Dawn Black for formatting this manuscript beautifully.

A NOVELLA

ANGEL

ONE
STRANGER

She gazed at the sky for probably the umpteenth time in the past hour.

It was a starry night. The North Star and the many known constellations stood out clearly, brightly. The moon was bright and perfectly spherical. There was no chance of rain.

It was the kind of night for romance, at least for a teenaged girl.

Stella Montero sat by herself at the street corner. The bench, with a newly dried coat of fresh paint, courtesy of a congressman, was right by the bus stop.

This was her favorite intersection, one she had grown up in. It was always brightly-lit by traffic lights and neon storefront signs. Green, red, orange, yellow and blue; it was its own kind of rainbow.

A gust of wind blew, stirring the street before her. Discarded newspapers and fliers flew by, tumbling on the stone pavement decorated by graffiti as colorful as the lights overhead.

Stella looked at the sky again. In mere seconds, it seemed to have grown murky and cloudy, as if someone had stolen the lights.

The stars were not the only ones that disappeared that night. Her hopes had gone, too.

Was it only this afternoon when Aaron called and asked if she wanted to go to the movies with him? Was it only a few hours ago when she, drifting on fluffy white clouds, had put on her best dress and favorite shoes and snuck into her mother's room to use her makeup and perfume?

She had already fallen from those clouds. More like stumbled, fell, and landed on the cold hard ground on her ass.

Six-thirty, the time she was supposed to meet Aaron Soler, had come and gone.

It was getting cold. She looked at her watch. It was already half past eight. She pulled her now-rumpled white cardigan more tightly around her body, shoving her hands into their shallow pockets. She would be an idiot if she allowed herself any more hope that he would show up at all. She had more self-respect than that.

"Stood you up, hasn't he?" The voice came out of nowhere, causing her to nearly jump out of her skin.

She sprang to her feet and backed a few feet away, hands clenching into fists as she turned to face the owner of the voice.

She had a box cutter in her bag, she thought, comforted. A girl who grew up in a city like hers knew how to protect herself.

He emerged from underneath the awning of an ice cream shop.

It was a boy. No, a man, tall and dangerous-looking as any predator of the shadows.

He had a thick mane of hair that fell past his shoulders. His skin was duskier than most, allowing him to blend easier into the night. Most of his face was still shrouded in the darkness; what she could see was about a third of his profile, sharp and harsh.

He was the most fearsome and compelling sight she had ever laid eyes on.

"Who are you?" It was almost a shriek, nothing like her own voice. "What do you want?"

He advanced into the light. His face looked even harder and older. There was a scar that ran the length of his right cheek, hidden in part by his long hair. He appeared to be in his early twenties, perhaps older.

"My name is Trey," he said, almost formally. "Hello, Stella."

She backed further away, hot and cold rushing through her veins at the same time.

"How did you know my name?" she demanded.

He gave a slight shrug, his shoulders rippling. "I asked."

She drew herself to her full height of five-foot-five, enough to intimidate most boys her age. It would probably have no effect on him, seeing that he was much bigger, but there was no harm in trying to appear braver than she actually was. "Asked who?"

"The people here. Everyone knows you."

"The people?" she echoed, stumped.

"You see them every day."

She stared, trying to understand what he meant. *Them? The people?*

She blinked, slightly taken aback by the bright light coming out of the open doorway of the leather repair shop down the street. She shut her eyes for the briefest of moments. When she opened them, she saw the sweet old woman who ran the shop give her a smile and a friendly wave. Seconds later, someone else left the shop, the old man who did all the repairs by hand or using an ancient pedal machine.

She watched them lock up the shop and walk off.

She understood.

This was her intersection, her neighborhood, her city.

"Yes," she said, more to herself than to the stranger. "I see them every day."

"So you do."

She glared up at him, feeling infinitely more confident that she did minutes ago. "That doesn't explain why you're here, or what you want from me."

"With you? Nothing." Trey sat on the bench she had vacated, draping his arm over the back of the seat and extending his legs. With his dark shirt and jeans, he looked like a giant snake, coiled and poised to strike. "Why I'm here has everything to do with your friend, the pretty boy."

"Aaron?"

"We were tipped off by one of his sidekicks. They come here and pick up girls for their pot sessions. The last one didn't go so well. Joshua didn't want to be part of the repeat performance."

'Pretty boy' Aaron, who was supposed to be her date, was a senior and the most popular boy at their college. His father was the mayor of one of the smaller towns that bordered the city. Aaron always had a lot of boys in his entourage, mostly those from more affluent families; they moved around the school as if they owned it. Girls who got his attention instantly became the most popular ones at school. With her being only a freshman, his initial attentions had flattered Stella to no end.

"Joshua." She repeated the name, trying to jog her memory. "He's the one with the red car. He was supposed to pick me up tonight, with Aaron, and…" Her voice trailed off.

"Joshua Benitez won't be coming, either," he said. "As for Aaron Soler, let's just say his plans have changed."

Girls. Pot sessions. Repeat performance. His words kept echoing in her head as she stood stock-still on the sidewalk. This time, she shivered for real. The night breeze was nothing compared to the cold coming from within her

"Did you want to sit down?" Trey moved his arm out of the way and slid to one side of the bench.

Stella hurried over and plopped down next to him, before she collapsed from the sheer weight of information she was absorbing.

"How long has this…been going on?" So many questions popped into her head, but it was difficult to put them into words. This was the kind of urban cautionary tale picked up and sensationalized by late-night crime investigation shows. "How did you know about them? How the hell do I know you're even telling the truth?"

"I don't have to answer any of that, do I?" He leaned forward, placing his elbows on his thighs and clasping his massive hands between them. He turned his head and peered at her face. "Or would you really want me to?"

She found herself looking into his eyes. They were midnight-black, unblinking. Strangely, she felt no discomfort under his gaze; instead, she stared right back.

"I just wanted to go on a date with Aaron, you know," she said softly. "When he asked me out, I was on top of the world, everyone at school was looking at me. They all saw me. And Aaron…he actually knew who I was, he got my name right and everything."

"I'm sure he did." There was no sympathy or sarcasm in his voice. He sounded as if he didn't have to convince anyone of anything. "He knew Victoria, Yasmeen,

Jennifer and Grace very well, too. Unlike you, they never stood a chance."

Stella didn't know the other three, but Jennifer Ang was a sophomore Aaron had dated the previous semester. She was a beauty queen, slated to compete in the national circuit of pageants that coming summer. Shortly after Jennifer and Aaron broke up, Jennifer's parents, who both worked abroad, had pulled her out of college in the middle of the year and brought her with them to Singapore. There had been rumors of a pregnancy, a party blunder that displeased her sponsors and ruined her image, an expulsion notice that was kept quiet...

"I knew Jennifer," she said. "She's a beauty queen who used to go to my college. She was his girlfriend for a while. She left town end of last semester."

"She got lucky. Grace was from about six weeks ago; she was studying Political Science in the university across town. She sat where you are sitting now. They saw her here before she got in the car with Benitez. She's in rehab now."

The strange reality of it all was overwhelming. In a matter of hours, she had been stood up in what was supposed to be the biggest date of life, her great crush had become a junkie who was bad news for girls, and a stranger from out of nowhere had appeared to be some twisted version of a guardian angel.

"Do you know where Aaron is?"

There was a crooked smile at the corner of Trey's mouth. "Do I really have to answer that question? The less you know, the better for you."

"I can't just sit here without knowing anything," she insisted. "If you want me to at least believe in what you're trying to tell me, then give me some answers."

"Soler won't be able to come here tonight. He and his friend are both at the docks. I brought them there earlier. We're trying to get them to sing. If they're lucky, they would get a little beaten down. If not…" He shrugged. "It's not like they even cared about what would happen to those girls."

"And you…you got them there?"

"It's my job. I work for the man who decided to put them there and, at the same time, get you out of something you wouldn't want."

She sat next to him, trying to keep her breathing even. She had somehow stumbled straight into the plot of a cheap action movie. At any other time, this would have felt contrived, even cheesy.

But she felt nothing like that.

This was a close call, not a joke. She could have ended up like any of those girls.

At that moment, Stella wanted nothing more than to see her mother. If anything happened to her, she could not even imagine her mother's reaction, the pain it would cause her. Even thinking about it made her feel *guilty*.

"I think I want to go home," she said.

The intersection was almost empty except for a few pedestrians and the familiar nighttime vendors who sold peanuts, duck eggs and green mangoes from their baskets. Most of the stores were already closed for the night. She had been there for almost three hours.

"I'll walk you there." He stood up the same time she did. Side by side, she barely made it to his shoulder. "Or wait until you get into a taxi."

"That won't be necessary," she said, flustered. "I live a few blocks away, near the commercial port."

"You can walk on your own if you want. I'll follow, anyway, and make sure you get there."

At any other time, she would have found those words creepy. She would have felt uncomfortable at the very least.

Tonight, however, was the kind of night that brought creepy to shame. If anything, she was past creepy.

With Trey, there was no feeling of discomfort, only a sense of awareness that he was more intimidating than everyone and everything else around her.

"Fine," she said, thinking she would rather have someone like him walking her home, rather than the less impressive assurance provided by her box cutter. "Let's go."

TWO
CRIMINAL

She looked at the sky again, maybe for the seventh time in the past half hour.

It was still raining. It showed no signs of letting up.

Stella stood by the waiting shed next to the main gate of her college. She was still mercifully dry, if not for errant drops of rainwater, brought about by nasty gusts of wind, whipping against her skin and her white college uniform.

This wasn't rain, she thought. This was a full-blown storm, at least Signal Number Two.

Night had been upon them for hours, with clouds blotting out the sun since mid-afternoon. All the classes for the evening finished at seven-thirty. It was already past eight.

The campus would be locked up soon. She would have to brave the storm on foot and wade her way through the flooded streets if she didn't want to get kicked out or get stuck. It was only a matter of time before the water levels got too high, if the rain didn't stop.

It was a simple, straightforward plan. Out the school and through the city's main street, where there was better drainage. She could use the buildings as shelter and sprint the last few hundred meters home past the plaza and the church. She would be soaked to the bone and maybe even get sick, but at least she wouldn't freeze to death outside her own school.

She turned to the other students huddled next to her, looking them over as she took off her shoes. There were three other girls and two boys, all looking as if they had the same predicament as she: brave the rain and flood, or wait it out. Her own choice already decided, she put her shoes in her bag and gave them a silent nod before walking out into the downpour.

It was easy enough to cross the road and make her way past the market. She was able to take shelter in the windows and awnings, up to and until she reached the main street.

By the time she made it to the intersection, the rain was so heavy she could barely see past a few steps in front of her. The shops had closed, with most of their lights and signs put out. What little light there was came from the streetlamps that still worked. She could feel water, cold and sticky, running in quick tiny currents under her feet. Blasted on all sides by strong winds, she could barely stay upright. It was like being in the middle of a sunken, vengeful city.

So much for her plan of using the buildings as shelter. She'd be lucky if she could make it past this junction. One wrong step could lead her into an open drainage hatch, if she didn't fall on her face, drown or get electrocuted first.

She stood in front of the sixty-year-old grocery store, squinting through the rain at a dim light coming from the window of a single shop across the street.

It was the old couple's leather repair shop. Were they still there? Could she possibly stay with them until this was over? Could she even cover that much ground without dying along the way?

Throwing caution literally to the winds, she drew her bag tighter against her body and sprinted full speed across the darkened road. Her bare feet burned from the roughness of the asphalt and the icy coldness of the flood.

"Hello? Can I please come in?" she called out, half-crashing, half-stumbling against the shop entrance. She pushed the wooden door open with all her strength and promptly ran into a wall.

She felt the wall give way a little, then something grabbed her upper arms, steadying her. It took her a second to figure out that she had run into someone, not something.

"Stella?"

It took a few more seconds for her eyes to adjust to the soft yellowish light inside the shop. Through a haze of stinging rainwater, she could make out a large black figure with equally dark hair and eyes. His face was the last thing that came into focus.

It was him.

"Trey?"

"What the hell are you doing here? Are you okay?"

She flinched at the harshness of his voice, or maybe at the strength of the grip he had on her. She could barely move her upper body.

At least she could still move her head. She nodded. "I'm fine. Can you please let go of me?"

His hands loosened and fell away. She watched him take a step back, inwardly debating with herself whether or not this was all real.

"Did I hurt you?" Without taking his eyes off her, he picked up something from the front counter. It was an emergency lantern, the source of light she had seen through the window. The shadows in the room shifted as he brought the lantern overhead.

"No, it's okay," she replied, a little too aware of how closely they stood to each other. The repair shop had always been tiny, but now it felt considerably cramped and tight. "Where's Auntie Yolly and Uncle Frank?"

"They've gone home. Did you come here to see them? All the shops closed hours ago." There was a note of disbelief in his voice.

She shook her head. "I was going to take shelter here. It was the only place with the lights on. I thought I could get home on foot, but the streets are too badly flooded."

Exhaustion and cold started nipping at her joints. She leaned against the wooden counter and put her bag on top. Her uniform was drenched, the skirt stained by the flood waters.

It was only then that she noticed it.

The blood.

Next to the space where she had put her bag, she spied small streaks of dark red liquid. Her eyes followed the stains over the side, all the way down the floor, to the spot where Auntie Yolly would usually stand to serve customers. Concealed behind the wooden counter were two limp bodies leaning against each other, their faces split open like overripe watermelons.

She screamed.

She tried but never got the chance. He put his arm around her and brought her close to him, pressing her so tightly against his body that any sound she could make was muffled against his chest.

"Stella," he said, very calmly, almost soothingly. "Stella. Stella, look at me. Please don't scream. Just look at me."

She could feel her body shake violently at the gory sight she had just witnessed. She focused on his voice, the welcome heat of his body. She was fine. It was just blood. It wasn't her blood.

"Look at me, Stella," he repeated. "Don't scream. They're not dead. I won't hurt you."

Clutching at his shirt, she willed herself to open her eyes.

She could see, under the light of the lantern he held up, that he was looking at her, too, into her eyes. His own eyes smoldered like hot coals. She focused on them. He wouldn't hurt her.

"Good," he said. "Now breathe."

She breathed out, a long exhale that made her light-headed. She held on to him, kept her eyes locked onto the somehow comforting familiarity of his face, as she tried to get her bearings.

"Please get me out of here," she heard herself say, trying very hard not to think of the bloody pulps next to her.

His face impassive, he let go of her and moved to the entrance to bolt it shut from the inside. When he was done, he gestured for her to go further inside the shop. "Let's go upstairs. If the water gets any higher, we'll be safer there."

Still feeling sick to her stomach, Stella carefully took her bag and did as instructed. Beyond the front of the shop, behind a thin plastic curtain, was the small workroom she was familiar with, lined wall to wall with tools and Uncle Frank's ancient pedal machine. To one side was a narrow flight of steps.

Guided by the light of the lantern, she was able to find her way to the mezzanine in record time. It was no larger than the downstairs area but had a higher ceiling. It appeared to be some kind of storage room for the shop's supplies. At one end of the room was a large glass window.

She put her bag on a shelf and made her way to the window. There was almost nothing to see, except the rain pelting against the glass and a very limited view of the flooded street outside. Most of the working streetlamps she saw earlier had gone out.

"You should sit down." Trey had put down the lamp on a tiny table and was bringing over a wooden stool for her. "You didn't have to see what you just saw. I guess you'd want an explanation?"

She settled on the stool, stretching out her legs and bare feet. She looked at him as he backed up and settled his large frame on the table next to the lamp. He looked bigger than she remembered; his hair was longer, too.

It didn't surprise her that he was talking so casually about the scene downstairs.

"Did you do that to them?" she asked, boldly.

"I did, just before you got here," he answered. "As I said, they're not dead. They're just out. I remember doing the same thing to your old friends a while back."

She remembered that night vividly. After she'd reached home, she had looked over her shoulder to see Trey gone. She had tried not to think about what had happened and had not told anyone, not even her mother. In the Monday that followed, there had been a large ruckus at the college about the two boys and the rest of their circle getting arrested. None of their gang of nine ever made it back to campus. As far as she'd heard, the other boys had been caught in the act of using drugs and hurting girls from other schools. Stella had thought that maybe Joshua had sung a little too well, or maybe Trey and his boss had made him do so.

"What did they do this time? Drugs?" Stella tried not to think of all the blood splattered on the counter and the floor.

"They were going to burn this building down. They got into the shop by breaking the front lock. They probably wanted to make it look like an accident that started from here, with the amount of leather oil they were carrying. They could have easily taken out this entire block, too. These buildings may look like solid stone from the outside, but inside it's all old wood."

"Why would they want to do that?" She thought of all the people who had stores in the block. She had known most of them since she was little; if not by name, she recognized them by face.

"Territory. Those fuckers are not from here, they're not even from Visayas. They're the Zamora family from Manila. They want to control the Pier District, starting with the small businesses. With the livelihood of the people gone, it would be easier to buy them out."

Trey got off the table and walked the length of the room to look out the window himself. "They tried the same thing last month at the port, with the vendor stalls. We barely got there on time. Otherwise, they could have burned down nearly two hundred stalls and parts of the commercial port."

She lived there. Her house was a stone's throw away from those stalls. She used to eat there regularly. "The only thing I heard about the port was that there was a huge riot that broke out among drunks over videoke. It was all over the news last month. My mother warned me not to go there in the evenings once they start all the singing and drinking."

He looked over his shoulder at her. "It was a good story, wasn't it? The boys staged the riot so well and got all the attention. We were lucky at the time."

She hesitated before asking her next question. "What are you going to do about them?" She gestured vaguely downwards.

"We're tracking down their friends who could be in the other buildings. As soon as we could get through the flood, we're taking these sons of bitches to their quarters across town. It took us a while to find out where they're holed up. Turns out they live in the house of Greg Garces. He's got ties with the Filipino-American mafia. I wouldn't be surprised if he's the one funding this little takeover attempt."

Another cause, another enemy.

More blood.

Why Trey did what he was doing she had no idea. "What do they want from the Pier District? I've lived here all my life. Most of us in our neighborhood have. It's just boats and warehouses and shops, and tiny old houses like mine."

He turned to face her completely. "Whoever controls the district controls the shipping routes and traffic. What goes in, what goes out, what everybody does in it. Most importantly, who gets to do business. All kinds of business."

"Somebody already does that, right?" She searched her memory for the name. It was a very old name, the elusive but notorious family that owned at least half of the district where she lived. "The Esguerras?"

"Raphael Esguerra. Ever since he took over a few years ago, other families and groups have been trying to take him down on all sides. A new leader usually takes a lot of heat. We've been putting out fires for a while now."

"You do dangerous things" she said. "You could get killed. Can't you just…quit?"

"And do what?"

"I don't know. Live and work somewhere else."

"Some of us can't just quit," he said with more emotion than she'd ever heard. "Some of us can't just give up the life we were born into. I grew up in the docks. I've lived here my whole life, too, just like you. I will do everything in my power to keep the Pier District from getting destroyed by outsiders, even if it means becoming a criminal to get rid of the people in my way."

His eyes left her then, as he focused his attention back to the window.

She stood up and picked her way over to the window, to see what he was looking at. It was still windy and raining heavily.

"I hope it stops raining soon. I want to go home. I've been at school since eight this morning."

"Aren't you cold? You look like you're going to be sick soon." The concern on his face made her aware of their closeness.

All she had to do was reach out, to touch him, to make sure he was real.

Ever since that night at the intersection, she had thought about him constantly, wondering if he ever existed at all. She had wanted to ask others about him, but had decided not to. She knew if he'd been just a figment of her imagination she would be devastated.

She was soaked with rainwater and freezing all the way to her insides. She wasn't even aware she had wrapped her own arms around her body to keep herself warm.

"I'm fine. It was my fault. I forgot my umbrella at the library. By the time I came back to get it, I was too late."

"Here." Trey started unbuttoning his shirt. She stared, heat rushing to her face. She tried to move her legs, to step away from him, but she was frozen to the spot. His black shirt opened, showing a grey t-shirt underneath. He took off the polo and handed it to her. "Put this on."

She was blushing and she knew it. The grey shirt had a tighter fit on his body. His shoulders and chest were broad, contrasting with his flat stomach and narrow hips. His black polo ended up in her shaky hand.

"Thanks," she heard herself choke out.

"I'm sorry if there are any…stains on it. I don't have anything warmer."

His shirt was the warmest thing she had ever touched. It had a clean, fresh scent, something like pine, tinged with the sea. She slid her arms into the shirt, almost disappearing into its considerably larger size.

"It's fine. It's very warm. Thank you."

They both stood by the window in silence, staring out into the rain and the nearly invisible city street.

"How are you, Stella?" It had gotten so quiet, his voice almost startled her. "I didn't get to ask you earlier."

"Life goes on, I suppose," she said. "School has been busier since I was a freshman. Thankfully, no one tried anything since that night. I think everyone got a little bit scared with what happened to Aaron and Joshua."

"A little bit scared?"

"Scared shitless, then?"

"Better."

She smiled. "So, how are you?"

He held up his left hand to the light. His knuckles looked freshly skinned, with a little blood caked and dried on them. "Bloody after my little fun. I guess I'm fine."

She was tempted to reach out and touch his hand. She could only clench her own fingers into a tight fist.

"I don't think I ever got to say thank you," she said.

"For what?"

"For back then." She could feel herself blushing again. She really had to get herself under control. All this caused by someone she barely knew, someone who had the knack of appearing out of the darkness for her, whenever she needed it most. "And for now, I think."

He shook his head. "You're thanking me for showing you two half-dead bodies in a leather repair shop?"

"For being there, Trey. It means something to me, even if the thought had never crossed your mind. Don't be like that."

She was rewarded with the tiniest of smiles. "This is as much of a surprise to me as it is to you, Stella."

The moment was interrupted by his phone ringing. He took it out of his pocket and answered. "Yes. I'm still here. Are you sure there's no one else out there?"

Trey looked out the window again. "Can you drop someone off first, then come back? Good."

"There's a car on the way," he said to her, replacing the phone in his pocket. "It can get through the flood. They'll take you home."

"That's great. Thanks." She looked around her, never at him. He would disappear again for goodness knew how long. She had to say it. "Will I see you again?"

He was already making his way back to retrieve the lamp from the table. He stopped mid-step and stared at her from over his shoulder. "What?"

"Will I ever get to see you again?" she repeated, as bravely as she could.

"Why would you want to see me? People don't usually like seeing me."

"I like seeing you," she retorted.

"Give me your phone." He walked back to her and held out his hand.

She reached into her bag, between rows of damp notebooks, and retrieved her phone. It was only slightly damp on the outside. The tiny device almost disappeared into his hand.

He looked at her phone's casing for a few seconds. It was made of shiny white silicone, decorated with a stylized drawing of a black archangel. He didn't comment. He turned it over to the screen side and started typing.

She heard his phone ringing again. "That's you calling. I'll save your number. Call me whenever you need, okay? I will answer."

She was tempted to say something in response when he handed the phone back to her. Nothing came out of her mouth. Not even when she retrieved her bag and followed him down the stairs.

She stood as close as she possibly could to the entrance, the farthest from the two bodies behind the counter. Trey was talking on his phone again, to someone else, about meeting them in another district across town.

It barely took any time before the car reached the flooded main street. She saw its headlights approaching and turned to him.

Stella finally found her voice. "Thanks." She took off his shirt and handed it back.

He shook his head. "No, keep it."

"I don't think I can." *Even if she wanted to.* "My mother will ask a lot of questions. It's a very small house. And it's just the two of us."

"Don't worry. I understand." He took the shirt and put it back on just as she heard a muted honking from outside. He unlocked the shop's front door and held it open for her. "Take care of yourself."

"You, too." She walked past him and stepped back into the street. Once outside, she could see that the rain had calmed down. It was still pouring heavily, but she could barely feel the wind.

He followed her. "Tell Mario where you want to go. He'll drive you there."

A dark four-wheel drive had stopped outside the shop. It stood amidst the flood looking like a tank. A middle-aged man rolled down the window by the driver's side and was about to step out when Trey held up a hand and opened the backseat door himself.

"Good night, Stella." The rain dripped on his face and hair. He didn't even blink.

She finally reached out and got to touch his left hand, the one with the skinned knuckles. It felt warm, rough, strong. "Thanks again. Good night."

He nodded and shut the car door. He didn't move from the spot where he stood, not even when the giant car pulled out of the sidewalk and started making its way through the flood.

She never took her eyes off him. Not until the sight of him was swallowed by the darkness that stretched out behind her.

THREE
FAREWELL

She looked up at the sky, then down at her watch. She sighed, trying to find a more comfortable position on the bench. Her legs and feet, clad in the black regulation stockings and low-heeled shoes of her school uniform, felt cramped. She felt warm in the white suit and regretted not changing into something cooler.

In the early evening, the intersection was the same as always, bright, messy and full of people rushing to catch a ride or selling food and trinkets. There was a thick, balmy breeze coming from the nearby waters of the docks, heavily tinged with salt. It was going to be a humid night.

Was it only a few years ago that she had sat on this same bench, shivering in a white cardigan, grappling with the dark realities of the world she was growing up in? It felt like a lifetime ago.

She wasn't surprised when someone suddenly took the spot next to her on the bench. She kind of expected it.

Stella had expected anything to happen since she got the text message from Trey last week. She had never called or messaged him in the past eighteen months since they last saw each other. She had not deleted his number, either.

It was the only message she had ever received from him.

Can we meet

Same place

Friday 6pm

She had called him back straightaway, just to make sure it wasn't someone else messing with her. He had answered after two rings, in that deep, raspy voice that sometimes followed her, especially when she walked alone in the city streets at night. Sometimes she dreamt of that voice, too.

For this Friday, she skipped her last class and told her friends she would meet them at the movies tomorrow evening. She had the foolproof reason of completing a report due that Monday.

"Hi, Stella." Trey, no longer a disembodied presence at the back of her head, looked surprisingly different. His long hair was tied back in a neat ponytail; he was dressed in a green polo shirt, blue jeans and brown shoes. He looked almost normal; his scarred face was as fierce-looking as ever, maybe even a little sharper with age.

Stella wondered how he thought she looked. She had definitely gotten taller since last time. Over the past few years, it was her height that brought her attention and sometimes opportunities neither she nor her mother had ever expected. A few months ago, she was approached by an events company to model for a local fashion show early next year.

"How are you, Trey?" she asked, politely. Light conversation had never been part of their interactions.

His Adam's apple was bobbing up and down. "I'm fine. Thanks for coming. I didn't think you would even answer my text. How have you been?"

She forced a smile, as strange as it felt to have normal small talk with him. "Good. Busy. Reports and exams take up most of my time. I'll be graduating this school year."

There was a rustle as he pulled out something from behind his back. She was certain he had gotten even bigger since last time; his shoulders looked wider in the more flattering cut and color of his shirt.

To her surprise, there was a small box of roses in his hands. There were three: one red, one pink and one white.

"I didn't know which color you liked, but I took a chance and picked roses," he said. "You always have on some kind of cologne that smells like roses."

"Yes, I like roses," she answered, taken aback. "Roses are nice."

If she had to list a hundred things this man was capable of doing, giving her roses would never even be a remote consideration, much less knowing how she actually smelled.

She reached out to take the box, trying to think of something else to say and failing miserably. She wasn't sure if she had intended to touch him, but her hands landed on top of his.

She looked up into his dark eyes and, sure enough, they were on her, too. She understood that look from a man, far better now than she did four years ago. No matter how mysterious he appeared to be, he was still a man, wasn't he?

"I wanted to see you," he finally said, breaking the silent, unmoving exchange between them. "I didn't want to leave town without telling you."

Her fingers closed around the box. It was made of white cardboard, plain yet sturdy, with a plastic display window to showcase the flowers inside. It was something she expected from someone like him: unadorned and straightforward.

"Where are you going?"

"Does it matter?"

"It does to me." She clutched the box closer to her, pressing it to the space between her chest and her stomach.

"I'm going to get a few things out of the way. North, mostly in Manila. We've lost a lot of good people to the Zamoras this past year. They haven't stopped trying to take over the Pier District."

His back heaved in what looked like a sigh. "It's only a matter of time before this escalates to an all-out war. But Iloilo is our home, we were born and raised here. We won't give it up, so we're bringing the war to them."

He was bringing the war to them, she thought.

Stella suddenly felt cold, empty, abandoned. The same way she had felt the first time she met him, on this very bench.

"You'll be back, right? You said before this is the life you were born into. You can't just leave, can you?"

There was that familiar tiny smile at the corner of his mouth. "It's not about leaving or staying. When I chose to do this, I knew I wouldn't be coming back. Sometimes, there are things we need to do that we can't just walk away from."

"I see," she said, evenly. "You'll be missing my graduation, then." It sounded stupid and pointless, but nothing ever made sense with him anyway. She could not even fathom how deep, dark and bloody the world he lived in was.

"I guess I will."

"I was a freshman when we first met, you know."

He nodded. "So, are you going to the senior prom with someone special?"

"Prom?" she echoed. "I haven't really thought about it. I don't have a special someone."

The idea had never really crossed her mind, not since what happened during freshman year. She had nothing against boys in general, but since then she had been averse to the young adult rituals of courting and dating.

Sure, there were a few boys who showed interest, some more than others. Darryl, whose family moved from another province at the start of their junior year, had been courting her shortly after he completed his first semester at the college. He was part of the student council and tutored younger students in Math subjects. Her mother liked him immensely. Stella didn't exactly dislike him; she just wasn't interested.

"It took me a while to trust boys again, after what happened. But I've learned a thing or two since then. I would stick an idiot in the throat with a box cutter before they could try anything funny." She had to smile through the heaviness in her muscles, a strange sensation considering how empty she felt inside.

They sat in silence for a while, before he stood up.

"I'm glad you're okay, Stella. At least I got one thing right in all of this."

Driven by a sudden sense of panic, she jumped to her own feet. "Are you going now?" she blurted out.

"I'm leaving tomorrow morning, so I'd better get ready." He was looking down at her with his mouth in a thin line. "I'm sorry if I bothered or upset you in any way. If there was someone I had to say goodbye to, it was you."

She felt something rise in her throat, bitter and painful and stinging hot.

Goodbye, she thought. It sounded so final and absolute.

Guardian angels were supposed to stay, weren't they? Wasn't he supposed to stay with her?

"I'm glad you told me," she said honestly. "It gave me a chance to see you. I thought I'd see you again sooner, after last time. But I'm glad you're here now."

"Me, too."

She swallowed hard, trying her best to stem the flood rising dangerously fast from within her. "It's early. I skipped my last class to meet you."

Before he could respond, she continued. "Let's eat something, okay? It will be my treat. I never had the chance to do anything for you."

Without giving him the opportunity to refuse, she grabbed him by the arm and pulled him through the throng of people milling the busy nighttime streets. She knew this place was part of him. This was home for Trey.

They had dinner of grilled fish and rice at a small, open-air eatery on the docks. It was nice to see him doing something normal with her, for a change.

Or for the last time.

It was almost nine in the evening when the lights of the stores and restaurants started going out, signaling the end of the day. She thought back to the time she had sat at the intersection and looked at the dying stars as her own hopes died, too.

Trey was the only constant presence between then and now, between an innocent teenager's disappointment and her first real heartbreak.

Her twisted kind of guardian angel, who was leaving her life as soon as the day was over. She was determined not to lose any more time she had left with this beguiling man.

"You live near here, don't you?" She had her hand on his arm, a gesture she had dared to try earlier, as they walked on the open pier, the area where smaller passenger boats docked in the daytime. She had thought he would not want to be touched, but she was wrong. She was glad to be wrong.

"It's near the old Customs office," he said, a little too formally, nodding towards a cluster of warehouses a block away. "My boss bought a few buildings here to keep some of the cars and for us to stay in if we wanted. I didn't want to live out of town."

"Can I see your place?" Heat flooded her face at her own boldness.

He stopped in his tracks. "It's late. I should be walking you home.

"I don't want to go home. Not yet."

"What do you want, then, Stella?"

Before her mind realized what she was doing, her body and heart had already made the call.

Her school bag, with his gift of roses, slid off her shoulder as she let go of his arm to, finally, put her own arms around him. She could reach his shoulders, his neck; she had to stand on tiptoes and force his head down with all her might. And it worked.

She kissed him.

FOUR
RECKONING

She didn't think about it anymore. She just moved as she had always wanted to. She ran her hands over his back and his thick hair; she used her tongue to taste him, his lips, the inside of his mouth. The rest of her followed; her chest and her hips pressed against him, wanting more, maybe at least for him to touch her, too.

He understood.

She knew as much when he came to life, knowing exactly what she wanted, what she needed.

His lips moved against hers; his tongue was deliciously soft and snake-like as it twisted its way into the depths of her mouth. His hands were all over her. His fingers ran through her long hair, his palms burned a path through her skin as he wrapped his arms around her waist and started caressing her buttocks. It wasn't very long until she was pressed against him so tightly, she could feel him, hard and insistent, against her own softness. His fingertips glided inside her skirt as he lifted one of her legs to wrap around his hip.

She gasped when he touched that part of her, expertly reaching inside the modest underwear she wore with her school uniform. His fingers rubbed and stroked her as she moaned against his chest.

She denied herself the pleasure that was beginning to build and decided to come back up for air. She grabbed at his arms, still feeling him against her.

"Take me home, Trey," she whispered into the night. "Make me yours."

He was always more at ease in the shadows. She watched as he picked up her things with ruthless efficiency. This time, it was his turn to take her hand and lead the way.

He lived in a warehouse, one filled with auto parts. The lighting was sparse; except for a few fluorescent bulbs, it was the lights of the pier that danced with the shadows. He locked the door behind him and led her to a tiny corner where stood a small table, a portable chest of plastic drawers, a tiny refrigerator, and his bed, wooden, with a thin mattress on top.

He did not say anything; neither did she. He brought her to the bed and made her stand before him. He undressed her then, unbuttoning her blouse and skirt first and sliding them off of her. He fumbled a bit with her bra, but when he finally undid the clasp and took it off, she blushed deeply as he brought his lips to her nipples and suckled them hungrily. She would have fallen to the floor, easily, had it not been for his firm grip around her body.

When he was done, he lowered her stockings and panties and, before she could protest, his lips, his tongue and his hands were on her, all over her. After a few moments, he lifted her to the bed, settling her gently on her back. His mouth came down between her legs again, as did his fingers, and she was at his mercy. She called his name, bucked her hips, spread herself further, dug her nails into his shoulders, until he brought her to the peak and she heard herself scream and moan in pleasure.

"You are so beautiful." She heard him speak huskily, from somewhere above her. It took a few seconds for her eyes to focus as she came down from what she knew was her first climax. She had read about it in romance novels, seen it in movies that made her blush, and even heard girls with boyfriends talk about it, but she had never expected it to feel like this.

She had never expected she would feel it with him.

In what little light there was, she could see him next to her on the bed, his dark eyes almost disappearing into the shadows. He was still fully clothed.

"Oh." Embarrassment sank in for the first time. Her hands came up, to cover her utter lack of modesty, but his fingertips were on her face before she could reach for something, like a blanket or pillow, to cover up with.

"You don't have to hide. Never from me." For the first time, she heard a tremble in his voice. She could barely see his face. His fingertips were gentle as he traced her cheeks; the skin on his hands was hard, rough and warm. She could smell herself in his touch.

She reached for him. Before she could wrap her arms around him again, he caught her wrists.

"I think it's time for you to go home." There it was again, the shakiness in his voice. "I'll walk you there." He slowly let her go.

"No," she said, trying to lift her torso, to get a better look at him. "I want to stay with you."

He hesitated, then sat up, the cot creaking under his weight. "This is your…first time, isn't it?"

"Yes." Was there something she had done he didn't like? "What does that have to do with anything?"

"This is the biggest mistake you could ever make." His back was as stiff and unyielding as a mountain, his voice low and almost menacing.

"Mistake? Who made you responsible for my decisions?" Heat rushed to her cheeks and forehead. She grabbed at the thin striped blanket folded under the pillow she had been lying on and hastily wrapped it around her nakedness.

"Decision? You call this a decision? To sleep with me?"

"To be with you, Trey." She was close to tears. She slid off the bed and got to her feet. He still had his back turned to her. At least he couldn't see her so disheveled and hurt. "I want to be with you. It was my choice to make. Don't you dare tell me you didn't want it, too. I felt it. Don't you fucking dare deny it."

He put his hands on his thick legs and rose, almost painstakingly. "I'm not denying anything." He turned slowly, running his fingers through his hair, which had become half-unbound after their kisses. He kept his eyes hooded, gaze to the floor, or at least not on her.

"I've never wanted a woman as much as I want you. Look at you, Stella. How could I or any man say no to you?"

"Then don't."

"If only it were that simple. If only I were any other man."

"You will never be any other man," she said, almost impatiently. "Look at you, Trey. How could any man compare to you?"

"Any other man wouldn't leave you." It was almost a whisper.

That stopped her.

"Then come back." Her lips finally uttered the very thing her heart had known for a long time. "When all this is over, come back to me."

As soon as she finished saying the words, a lone tear slid down the corner of her left eye, landing and splashing on her naked shoulder. She was terrified he saw it.

That was the last shred of her dignity.

Somehow, that was also the last shred of his control.

As long as it took her to blink back more tears, he closed the distance between them. The way he grabbed hold of her around the waist was almost bone-breaking, crushing the breath out of her. His lips came down on hers like a clap of thunder, as powerful and overwhelming as he.

Her flimsy cover of a blanket fell to the floor, just as she gave him her complete surrender. This time, there was no waiting, no caressing, no gentleness, as she kissed him back like a woman starved.

Dimly, she felt her hands rip away at the last barriers between them, his clothing. It didn't take long for him to be just as naked as she. He looked beautifully inhuman in the dim light and shifting shadows; his skin was smooth where there were no scars, but he had dozens of them all over his body, mixed with what looked and felt like burn marks. His hair fell on her face like a velvet curtain, scented by the sea and his sweat.

They didn't even make it to the bed, or at least she did, halfway. He was inside her, a perfect fit, buried completely, as her legs went around his waist, his shadow looming over her. She felt him thrusting faster and harder by the second, heard him say her name again and again, and, finally, asked her to look at him.

Their eyes locked briefly, and she drowned at the ferocity and desire she saw in the way he looked at her, and his lips were on hers again. He thrust the hardest then, and he shouted as his body shook as if he had a hundred earthquakes inside him, from inside her.

He collapsed, draped across her, his hair and sweat and breath on her breasts. She could feel a slick wetness burning straight from him into her.

Her heart was pounding so loudly she could barely hear anything else. She put her arms around him and kissed the top of his head, feeling only tenderness as she watched him looking spent and vulnerable.

Is this how it was supposed to feel?

She never had any more time to think about it that night. She could only feel, only him. They made love again, and again, and once more. He was insatiable, as if he wanted every last part of her for himself, but, to her surprise, so was she.

By dawn, he had touched and kissed every inch of her, and she of him. She was straddling him, arms around his neck, his teeth and tongue on her nipples, when she saw the first strains of light filter in through the high windows of the warehouse. By the time she came in his embrace, moaning his name, morning was upon them.

He was on his back and she sprawled on top of him, nuzzling his chest, when she realized it was the first time she was seeing him in the light of day.

"Come back to me, Trey," she blurted out, afraid he would somehow disappear. "No matter what happens, just come back to me."

He didn't respond, not for a long time. His arms went around her, so tightly, so protectively. She felt his lips on her temple, his heartbeat in her ear, his hands in her hair. She took these in, every touch, every scent, every sound, every feeling.

"I love you, Stella," he finally said.

FIVE
PRISON

I love you.

After he said the words, he slowly moved her to the bed and wrapped her in his blanket. She watched him dress in his usual dark clothing and take only a black backpack.

"It's yours now," he said, giving her the keys he had used the night before. "Do whatever you like."

Before she could protest, he brought his arms around her and kissed her deeply. With one last caress on her cheek and her hair, he was gone.

Trey.

She didn't even know his last name.

Stella got out of his bed, dressed and gathered her things. It was only when she finished locking up the warehouse that she felt the scalding pain in her throat, from last night, finally bubble to the surface, unleashing itself with her tears.

As she walked home, she didn't have the heart to check her phone, knowing that it was probably bursting with worried texts and missed calls from her mother. She would deal with it all later. All that mattered at the moment was she make it through the pain, see herself home alive.

She had no idea how hard she had been clutching his box of roses in her hands. She was just about to cross the intersection when it fell from her grasp. The box burst open, spilling the three roses onto the street, along with a small rectangle of paper.

She crouched down and slowly gathered the fallen items, fitting them into her school bag, feeling spent and raw as she did. The rectangle turned out to be a business card, with something written on the back of it by hand. The name was familiar.

RAPHAEL I. ESGUERRA, III

Chief Executive Officer

Esguerra Holdings

Trey's boss. There was a number printed underneath, which looked oddly familiar. It took her a few seconds to figure out that the mobile phone number was Trey's. She had looked at his number and only message from last week so many times.

Why was his phone number on his boss' card?

At the back of the paper, in bold, slashing handwriting, was a short message.

Call whenever you need.
There will be an answer.

Trey

Unable to make sense of what she had just read, she fumbled with the rest of her things and slowly sat down at the bench by the intersection, taking deep breaths.

She slowly went back in memory, to what he had said in the time she was with him.

"Iloilo is our home, we were born and raised here. We won't give it up, so we're bringing the war to them."

"I work for the man who decided to put them there and, at the same time, get you out of something you wouldn't want."

"When I chose to do this, I knew I wouldn't be coming back."

"Some of us can't just quit. Some of us can't just give up the life we were born into."

Was Trey the boss he was referring to? Was he actually Raphael Esguerra?

Was he the Raphael Esguerra who protected her city?

Unable to stop herself, she took out her phone. The screen showed eighteen missed calls and almost double in unread messages. The battery was down to twelve percent. She scrolled through her contacts, found Trey's number, and called it. She felt an icy chill envelop her body, despite the warmth of the morning sun.

Her call was picked up after two rings.

"Hello, Miss Montero. Good morning." The voice was different, older, female. It sounded almost like her own mother's voice.

"Hello," Stella echoed. She suddenly felt disoriented. "Who's this? Is Trey there?"

"My name is Rhoda, Miss Montero. I work for Mister Esguerra. Is there something I can do for you?"

"Where's Trey? I want to talk to him. Please."

"I believe he has informed you he will be indisposed. He has given us instructions to be at your service, as and when you need."

Us? Her brain tried to cope with the words of the woman at the other end of the line. *At her service?*

Wherever Trey was, she had already gotten her answer.

"No, thanks," she heard herself say. "I just wanted to give him back the keys to his... house."

"Did you? I was under the impression he has given them to you, to access and use the warehouse as you please."

"No. Yes. I didn't understand what he was trying to tell me."

There was a pause from Rhoda. "Is there anything else you need, Miss Montero? I can send a car for you if you need to get somewhere, wherever you are in the city."

To her horror, Stella felt a few tears slowly escape her already stinging, sleepless eyes. "I don't need a car. I'll walk home."

"Very well, Miss Montero. Please call me if you need anything, anything at all."

"Goodbye, Rhoda." Stella disconnected the call. She mechanically picked up her bag and stood up. She could feel her legs extend unwillingly, still sore from her night with him. She was beyond tired.

Raphael Esguerra.

A powerful name, feared and respected in the world she lived in.

Trey.

The man who moved in and out of the shadows and into her life, into her darkest dreams and desires.

They were the same person. The only man she had given her heart and her body to.

She would have given anything to make him stay. She knew, however, that no one could tell someone like Raphael Esguerra what to do.

The very same person who told her he loved her.

She had never said she loved him, too, had she? Loved him the moment she first laid eyes on him all those years ago, stepping out of the darkness, under the bright neon lights of a street corner.

It was the only regret she had. It was a prison she willingly put her heart into.

She carried this regret in the days, weeks and months that followed, silently, guardedly.

When she reached home that Saturday morning, instead of greeting her with panic or anger, her mother told her that she received a visitor named Rhoda, the mother of one of Stella's classmates, earlier that morning. Rhoda had apologized for not calling to tell her that Stella was helping her daughter with an urgent term paper, help given at the last minute to a desperate classmate. After breakfast in a fast food restaurant with her daughter, Stella would be home.

She went to the movies that evening with her friends. On Monday, the student council started putting up posters for the senior prom, scheduled on Valentine's Day. She wasn't surprised to get asked by Darryl, whom she politely turned down. In the weeks that followed, she refused four more invitations.

It was almost Christmas when she first heard about it on the news.

It was hard to miss. A large explosion in Sampaloc, Manila had taken down almost four blocks of factories and warehouses. A hundred injured, twenty dead. Up to and until Christmas, there were interviews of a bereaved widow named Connie Zamora, clutching a brood of four children, mourning the death of her husband, business magnate Michael Zamora. Connie demanded justice for her family and the families of their employees.

The media and the police suspected terrorists trying to make a statement. Stella always looked at the sketches released to the public, but never found one she recognized.

Over the school break that December, just before New Year, she went back to the warehouse, on a quiet weekday evening.

It was the same way she had left it. She tidied up the bed, willing herself not to think of the person she had shared it with, and stripped the sheets for washing. She went through the plastic drawers and the refrigerator. The fridge had a few bottles of water and an unopened Snickers chocolate bar. The drawers contained an assortment of black and grey shirts, a few pairs of dark jeans, and shorts of different colors. All the clothes had been washed and neatly folded. In the bottom drawer was a plain ruled notebook and a few pencils. Nothing was written inside the notebook; there were only sketches that filled the pages, drawn in a neat, meticulous hand.

They were all sketches of her.

She spent the next hour crying on his bare mattress.

In January, she walked the runway for the first time, in a Dinagyang Festival fashion show. The designer was so impressed that she offered to design Stella's gown for the latter's senior prom, as part of her Valentine's Day portfolio.

February came with typhoons, one after the other. The rain on Valentine's Day reminded Stella of that night two years ago when the city was flooded.

The prom was at a seaside resort across town, in a covered pavilion with tall, thick glass windows that overlooked the beach. In spite of the weather, almost all her classmates and their dates had come.

Stella arrived with two other senior girls who didn't have escorts like her. All three of them lived in the same area and had opted to travel to and from the event together.

She made a stop at the bathroom before entering the venue. Pictures of the night were very important, according to the designer. They had contracted one of the prom photographers to take additional photos of her wearing the new dress.

The gown was made of deep red velvet, the color of blood. The neckline was cut low, off the shoulders, with small crisscrossing straps around her upper arms. The rest of the fabric was molded to her bodice and hips, then came apart by her left thigh in a slit, showing off her long legs, with the hemline almost brushing the floor.

The hairdresser had styled her hair half down, half up. It fell in waves all the way to the middle of her bare back. She had asked for three small roses to be put around the loose ponytail on top of her head. One red, one pink, one white.

'I love you, Stella.'

The words had echoed in her mind, heart and soul countless times since she heard them, for the first, only and, possibly, last time.

Staring back at her in the mirror was the very image of a romantic heroine, draped in the colors of love.

But she wasn't that heroine.

She was Stella Montero, who didn't even have a date to the prom. She didn't have someone special. She already had something more than that.

She already had her prison.

SIX
STORM

The prom was meant to last past midnight. The weather had other plans.

At nearly eleven that evening, Stella stood next to the glass door of the pavilion and looked up. She couldn't see any of the stars. The sky was almost completely covered in thick clouds. There was only the moon, cutting through the dark shroud with tiny yet sharp slivers of light.

The rain fell in a steady downpour, the winds picking up in speed with each hour that passed. A full-blown storm would be upon them soon.

She had spent the past few hours having her picture taken and getting congratulated by practically everyone present: her teachers, classmates and schoolmates, even visitors from other schools. She was, apparently, the frontrunner for Prom Queen.

She was not surprised when someone from the student council came over to escort her across the dance floor. It was the treasurer, a classmate of hers since freshman year named Vic. He guided her up the small stage and led her to a spot in a line where three other girls stood. Vic winked at her and mouthed, *"Congratulations. It's you."*

In one corner of the platform stood the male half of the prom court. Darryl already had the Prom King crown on his head. He was flanked by three other boys from her class who wore blue sashes as the first, second and third princes.

The emcee, a deejay from a popular local radio station, came forward dramatically, brandishing an important-looking cream-colored envelope. He took out a card of the same color and began to read out the names of the third and second princesses.

Stella felt the hug of the last girl standing next to her seconds after she heard her name being called as Prom Queen. The president of the student council came forward and put a pink and gold sash over her shoulder, followed by the college dean who pinned a bejeweled tiara to her hair. She was hugged and kissed by a few more people before Darryl stood in front of her bearing a bouquet of white, yellow and pink flowers, mostly roses.

Photographers surged forward and snapped pictures at an alarming, blinding rate.

She could hear the strains of David Pomeranz's song, 'King and Queen of Hearts,' coming over the speakers. This was the traditional Prom King and Queen dance.

The crowd applauded. The catcalls, whistles and whoops were deafening.

The skies responded, splitting open with a resounding, bright burst of lightning. Thunder followed, echoing through the sudden darkness that blanketed the entire pavilion.

"The power just went out," she heard the deejay say loudly. "Everyone please stay calm."

Someone grabbed her hand, pulling her to the left side of the stage. She thought at first it was Darryl, but she was certain he was on the opposite side of the stage, where moments before he stood under the spotlight with an obnoxious-looking bouquet in his hand and a silly grin on his face.

Stella found her voice, her hand instinctively going up to prevent the tiara on her head from falling. She could use it as a weapon, too, just in case.

"What the hell do you think you're doing?" she demanded.

"Hi, Stella." The voice came from the deepest shadows of stage left, the only sound she could hear clearly even with the rising din of people talking in the darkness.

She knew that voice.

"Trey?" she heard herself respond, in what sounded like a desperate whisper. Maybe she had completely lost it now.

Cellphones and lighters began coming to life on the pavilion floor, allowing her to see more clearly.

A single streak of light moved across the spot where she heard his voice coming from, falling on his profile for the briefest moment.

That was all she needed to see.

She unceremoniously pulled the errant tiara off her head and tossed it aside, then jumped off the stage and into his arms.

She landed on his chest, her fingers clutching the fabric of his shirt, her face burrowing into his neck, desperately taking in his familiar scent of pine and the sea.

Trey's hands were warm on her back. He was raining kisses on her hair and face. She knew the feeling of his lips on her skin.

"Let's get out of here," she heard him say.

Nothing in the world could stop her from going with him. She was not sure if he carried her, or she ran alongside him, but she found herself in a hut at the farthest end of the resort, cloaked by the night and the rain.

Before them, the surf crashed roughly against the shore. Their shelter of dried woven leaves made little consequence. They were both soaked to the skin.

It was only when he stood still before her, in the pale, thin light of the moon, was she finally convinced he was real. She reached out and touched his face, taking in all the planes and angles.

"I missed you so much," she said. "Whoever you are."

"It doesn't matter who I am. It never mattered to you."

He was right. It never did.

"What matters is that I love you." The words came out easily, as naturally as she breathed in the salty air and the heady scent of him. She touched the scar on his right cheek. She watched as he turned his head and started kissing her fingertips.

"You are so beautiful." His voice was equal parts passionate and tender, as was his gaze.

"So are you," she said, as she traced his lips and jawline.

"I came back to you," he said. "Do you know what that means?"

She put her arms around his torso, angling her ear so she could hear his heartbeat. "That you really love me? That you missed me, too?"

"It means I am yours, Stella. I have been yours the moment I saw you sitting in that intersection. I couldn't stop thinking about you. I tried to draw you. I never thought I could even touch you. You're an angel on earth I would die to protect."

She could feel the tears welling up behind her eyes, from the flood of emotion that overcame her.

But she didn't have time for tears now.

She only had time for him, because she belonged to him, too.

She reached up and put her hands on his shoulders, the same way she had all those months ago. She didn't have to pull him down. He lifted her off her feet to kiss her.

"I am yours, too," she said against his lips. "*Raphael. Trey.*"

She let the names roll off her tongue. There was nothing strange about them. They were both him.

Stella kissed him, then, before she finally called him what she had really wanted to, all these years.

"*My angel.*"

ABOUT THE AUTHOR

Shirley Siaton writes edgy and evocative stories and poems. Her worlds are in a deliciously dark cross-section of the romance, neo-noir, action, fantasy, new adult and contemporary genres.

She has several books of fiction and poetry released since February 2023. Her first book is the free verse collection *'Black Cat and other poems.'* She also pens juvenile literature as Shirley Parabia.

She is an award-winning writer, poet and journalist in English, Filipino and Hiligaynon, lauded by the Stevan Javellana Foundation, Philippine Information Agency and West Visayas State University. Her essays, short stories and poems have been published internationally in print and digital media. Her multi-lingual plays have been staged in the Philippines.

Shirley is a black belt in Shotokan Karate and an international certified fitness coach. Originally from Iloilo City, she is based in the Middle East with her husband and two daughters.

LINKS

Shirley's official website:

shirleysiaton.com

Complete reading guide:

shirley.pub

Subscribe to Shirley's VIP list for free exclusive updates:

newsletter.shirleysiaton.com